Ensuring Your Place In Hell

This is a work of fiction. Names, characters, businesses, places, events and incidents are either the products of the author's imagination or used in a fictitious manner. Any resemblance to actual persons, living or dead, or actual events is purely coincidental.

Ensuring Your Place In Hell
First Edition May 2023
Edited By: Christine Morgan
Cover Illustration By: Kristina Osborn
(www.truborndesign.com)
Wrap By: Christy Aldridge (Grim Poppy Design)

Copyright © 2023 Stephen Cooper
Copyright © 2023 Otis Bateman
Copyright © 2023 Stuart Bray

All rights reserved. This book or any portion thereof may not be reproduced or used in any manner whatsoever without the express written permission of the publisher except for the use of brief quotations in a book review

Ensuring Your Place In Hell

Stories By:

Otis Bateman
Stuart Bray
Stephen Cooper

Splatploitation Press

This is your last chance to bail before things get really Fucked Up!

Splatploitation Press

www.splatploitation.com
https://www.youtube.com/@Splatploitation
https://splatploitation.substack.com

Home Movies from Hell

By Otis Bateman

Eric stared at his email's inbox, feeling like a ravenous man about to feast in only a matter of moments. He had been waiting months anxiously for a response, and here it finally was! With nervous trepidation, he excitedly opened the email and began to read.

Dear Eric,

It is with immense pleasure that we here at Hurt 2 The Core Productions welcome you to our ever-growing roster of content creators! Your animal hurtcore video, Drill Dog, was absolutely depraved and really got the attention of me and my staff!

At H2TC, we strongly believe in quality over quantity, and pay as such. We are on the lookout for films that feature the long, painful death of young children. If it is your predilection, we also procure child pornography, and pay the highest price for high quality videos of that ilk. We pay top dollar for attractive females butchered on celluloid as well, albeit slightly less than for female children; we have quite the fanbase for those films.

We will accept male deaths, but here's the caveat: it must be brutal and/or sensational. It will of course be the lowest payout, as it is the least popular service we offer to our fan base.

Once again, we thank you for reaching out to our syndicate and we look forward to hopefully working with you in some capacity. We cannot wait to see what you send us.

Sincerely,
Peter Scully, Owner H2TC

And there it was! Eric's hero, Peter Scully, had taken the time to write back to him! The creator of the most infamous video on the deep web, Daisy's Destruction! Eric felt a euphoric ecstasy wash over him in warm waves, causing him to involuntary shiver in delicious delight.

In the video he had affectionately dubbed "Drill Dog," he had taken a Pomeranian puppy and lightly crushed it at first, not enough to maim or kill it of course, just to scare it and cause discomfort. The puppy's yelps of distress harshly filled the previously silent soundtrack. Next, Eric procured a DeWalt drill with a six-inch drill bit attached to it. He grabbed the puppy in his right hand by the scruff of the little rat's neck, and with his dominant left, he unceremoniously slammed the bit into its puckered asshole with absolutely no lubrication whatsoever. The savage act caused the dog to squawk in pain like it had been zapped with electricity. Eric pressed the button, causing the drill to buzz to vibrant life, swirling the pup's guts like a macabre blender.

The pain was brilliant, like a poisonous inspiration. The puppy bucked against Eric's iron-clad grip to no avail as he continued drilling its insides into Swiss cheese. A deluge of blood and shit gushed from its ruined anal cavity, coating the drill as well as Eric's hand in gooey-shit-blood-gruel. As he began extracting the drill, he found that the puppy's intestines had become hopelessly entwined in the gore-caked drill bit. The puppy howled in pure, unadulterated agony as Eric drew the drill's remaining inches from its ruined sphincter, its intestines stretching to the outermost limits possible, like mozzarella cheese on a piping hot pizza pie.

Eric had then dropped the shell-shocked pooch onto the ground and used his foot to hold it in place as he took out a fillet knife and started hacking off its legs, just for cruel spite. The dog somehow managed to drag itself across the ground as best as it could, even with most of its limbs now missing or horribly mangled. It left a trail of blood behind it like a slug's oozing trail.

As a final act of cruelty, he began applying pressure on its head with his foot. As he heaped on more torque, the dog's eyes painfully bulged from their sockets, blood jetting from its mouth, eyes, and nose in steaming freshets.

And that was that. He'd submitted the video in hopes of garnering the attention of H2TC, and it had worked like a charm! They were giving him a shot at the big leagues!

He had known for some time that he wanted destruction to be his profession, and the savage act of killing this dumb animal only cemented it further. But now he really had to wow these guys! No half-assed debauchery was going to do!

Eric glanced from his monitor toward the living room, where his friend Dylan was mercilessly killing a horde of demons in Doom Eternal, cursing like a drunken sailor as he blasted off limbs and obliterated skulls with the best weapon in the game: the BFG, aka, the big fucking gun.

"Take that you filthy cunts!" Dylan yelled at the screen.

"Hey bro, pause that, would you? I got some big news!"

"How very," Dylan said. "Spill the beans, bruh!"

"Come here man!"

Dylan trotted over, lighting a cigarette. A plume of smoke drifted lazily in the air, surrounding them in a shroud of smog.

"Here you go, read this and prepare to get HYPE!" Eric hooted.

Dylan quickly devoured the correspondence from H2TC, the expression on his face changing from mild curiosity to jubilation. He turned to Eric, beaming in rapturous joy at the possibilities of this wonderful news.

"So, we are really going to go through with this? Making snuff flicks, I mean?"

"Are you still down for the cause?" Eric asked.

"Does a bear shit in the woods?" Dylan said.

"Let me check my magic eight-ball; it says yes!"

"That's a BINGO!" Dylan laughed.

They chuckled at their little exchange before silently daydreaming of the putrid possibilities of this path they were planning to take. They both were fascinated with real gore sites, such as Death Addict and YNC, just to name a few. They constantly watched the vilest death videos they could find, on the clear as well as the dark web. Titillating fare such as Most Depraved Person on Planet Earth, How to Clear a Room In 90 Minutes, Misanthrope, and Amber Alert ... especially Amber Alert.

Before they had stumbled upon H2TC, Amber Alert was the hardest thing they'd seen floating around. It highlighted children being abused in all sorts of nefarious ways. It was evil, deliciously so.

But, once they had seen what true evil men could conjure up within the furthest reaches of the dark web, well, everything else got the mute button pressed on it afterwards.

Now they were being given the chance to rise into the upper echelons of depravity, and they weren't going to slack on slinging the red stuff. No way!

"Okay, you read the email, so you know they don't care about men, for the most part," Eric said. "It's children and women their buyers clamor for, so that's what we will try and deliver. If worse comes to worse, we can kill some dude but make it ultra brutal and nasty to make up for the gender."

"Yeah, I mean, we can just go all August Underground on some prick, and show these fuckers just how sick and repellent we can really be!" Dylan boasted.

"Hell yeah, broski, and I know just the place we can go hunting!"

"And where, pray tell, is that, my dude?" Dylan asked.

"The homeless camp at the edge of town. I bet there's

plenty of homeless hoes slinking around there. They have a bevy of brats clinging to their saggy titties, too! And you know what the best part is? No one will give two flying fucks that we are massacring them! Shit, they will probably give us a medal for cleaning up the neighborhood!"

"Dude, that's some brilliant Mark Twain shit!"

Eric gave a benevolent curtsy, as Dylan pantomimed the "we're not worthy" scene from Wayne's World.

"Let's get some grub and then head to the shed and procure our implements of hell so we can butcher some hogs!" Dylan said.

"It's like you are reading my mind; we're on some mind-meld type of shit." Eric said.

"Hopefully, luck is on our side and some juicy specimens will be there. If there are only a handful of stew bums then I am going to be Hella pissed!"

"We will just take it out on them, then, and make some art with their viscera. We can paint the forest with their blood!"

"Sounds like a plan Stan."

"Let's eat, first, though; I could go for a taco," Eric said.

***

Daisy's mother had been reluctant to let her move back home, after her boyfriend had left her to be with a stripper he had been seeing on the side. To add insult to injury, not only did they have a child out of wedlock -- Hazel, who had just turned ten -- but Daisy now had another baby on the way.

At thirty-eight weeks, it could be any time. Daisy didn't even know the gender of the child; she had wanted it to be a surprise for her and her boyfriend. Now, it only seemed like a cruel indictment for how callous the world could be.

Daisy'd wished she had somewhere, anywhere to go other than her mother's, but Hazel had been scared and hungry. She had stared dismally into her purse at the paltry sum of money in her pocketbook. One-hundred dollars, in crumpled, wrinkled bills to her name. That pittance wouldn't have gotten them very far.

So, she had done the only logical thing possible: swallowed her pride and called her mother to beg for a place to stay, just till she could get back on her feet.

Her mother, somewhat of a religious fanatic, had despised Daisy's life choices. Being a closet racist had also caused her to hate Daisy's boyfriend, Jesus, for his ethnicity. The play on his name and her mother's almost obsessive adoration for all things biblical had not been lost on her. It was even almost funny....

For a brief time, she and her mother had buried the hatchet, although tentatively. The handle had been left sticking out, just in case. Things had gone well for about a month, before Daisy's mother crumbled from the pressure of her pompous church group. How could you let a sinner back into your home, even if it is your daughter, they had hissed. And that was it. She had come home from Sunday service and requested that Daisy find somewhere else to go.

If it was just her, she would have told her pious priss of a mother to go to hell and storm out. But Hazel was in tears because she couldn't fathom why her grandmother was kicking her and her mother out into the streets.

"If it was just me, I could understand, Mom. But to do this to your granddaughter is just unfathomable." Daisy said, watching her mother angrily tossing clothes out of the second story window in a flustered fury.

The old woman chose her words carefully.

"You have been a disappointment to me since you were a child. I have prayed until my knees were raw that you would claw your way out of this hellish hole you have chosen to reside in your whole damned existence. I can't take what you have become, Daisy, and with you as Hazel's mother, I am certain the same outcome will befall her as well."

It was as if her mother had slapped her with an invisible hand. Daisy flinched back from her words like they were daggers with a jagged edge that sliced deeply into her.

"Grandma, please don't kick us out!" Hazel cried.

"Quiet, child; children should be seen and not heard!"

The look her mother gave Hazel turned Daisy's heart to stone. How could someone that claimed to be one with the Lord be such an utter shit?

"C'mon Hazel, let's get out of here; it's clear that we are not wanted here any longer."

"But, Mama, where will we go?"

"Wherever we want, kiddo!"

And with that Daisy and Hazel left the house, slamming the door behind them with a thunderous crash. Once outside, Daisy gathered what her mother had tossed out the window and stowed it inside a backpack that had been flung outside as well.

She led Hazel up the street, where they walked for a while until they stumbled upon a covered Metro bench. The wind had picked up and become blustery, causing them to quickly dig out their jackets to combat the sudden chill. Daisy wished she had a car, but Jesus had taken that with him. Typical, uncaring bastard that he was. He only cared about getting his dick wet; his family could go away for all he gave a damn.

Daisy plopped heavily onto the bench with a huff. Hazel saint daintily next to her, then scooched in as close as possible to absorb some much-needed warmth. Daisy looked down at her sweet daughter and bravely fought off a torrent of tears wanting to let loose. She wouldn't cry in front of Hazel. She would save that for later, after Hazel had fallen asleep.

Her main concern was what to do now. She had some money, yes, but it would go quickly, especially if she got a room for the night. Daisy's brain went into over-drive as she tried to figure out what to do for the short-term. So lost in thought was she, that she barely noticed the disheveled older man wandering over towards the bench.

"Hey, the last bus already came by, you two; you just

missed it," the man said.

Daisy's head jerked up in startled fright from the gruff voice so precariously close. What a fool she was! So lost in thought, she could be putting her daughter in danger! The streets were no place for a ten-year old to hang out on a dreary, chilly night.

"Oh really? Geez, thanks for letting us know, sir. I guess we better figure out something else then," Daisy said.

At that moment, their eyes met; Daisy's on the verge of spilling a deluge of tears, and his looking at her tenderly, almost paternal. He fished in his pocket and quietly handed her some Kleenex. She gave him a polite, thin smile in return.

"Look, miss, my name is Sid, and I know you don't know me from Adam, but if you need a place to go for the night, I have a tent set up in the woods. It's near to the homeless camp, but not, if that makes sense. I can get a roaring fire going in a jiffy and I scored myself two new cans of Hormel chili that I would be glad to share with you and your little one."

Daisy studied Sid. Although he had obviously lived a hard life, his eyes were not. They had a benevolent quality to them. She felt a vague sense of ease wash over her in waves. Sid reminded her of her father, in a way, before colon cancer had taken him away at much too young an age. She did not fear Sid, and something told her to trust him, so she did.

"What do you say Hazel, want some chili?" Daisy asked.

"Mmm, I would love some! I'm so hungry I could eat a horse!" Hazel chirped.

"Wow, a whole horse you say?" Sid teased.

"Yes sir!" Hazel said.

"No need to call me sir, little lady. Just call me Sid."

"Okay, Sid!"

"Well, ramblers, let's get rambling!" Sid said.

"Lead the way Sid!" Hazel giggled.

"Yeah, it's chili time; my belly is already growling in anticipation!" Daisy laughed.

They headed towards the camp, the three of them talking happily to one another about this and that, all troubles momentarily forgotten.

***

But a new, far deadlier problem was heading in the exact direction as they were treading…

***

Eric and Dylan decided to park a distance away from the camp, just to be safe. They were young and psychotic, to be sure; totally stupid, they were not.

Most of their young lives had been spent watching shows like Forensic Files and listening to true crime podcasts. These avenues of entertainment bore strange fruit, the kind that helped the attentive watcher or listener evade detection if they were wily enough and took enough notes. They both were staunch believers in giving it their all when it came to their passions, and murder was a huge part of their lives, especially now that they were pursuing it as their career choice.

Eric found a desolate, muddy road that was obscured by trees and pulled down the narrow, murky lane and parked.

They sat quietly in the car for a moment, no doubt mutually thinking of the impending carnage about to unfold by their very hands. A giddy euphoria had them in a rapturous stupor.

"Let's put on our GoPro head straps and QuickClips right now so we don't forget," Eric commanded.

"Yes, boss!" Dylan mocked.

Both grabbed their respective peripheral devices and affixed them in place.

"Dude, I want to murder the world!" Dylan said.

"Bro, same. I can't wait to mutilate some hobos. Maybe we will get lucky and find some pauper pussy to pummel!"

"Dare to dream, bruh!" Dylan said.

"I bet a homeless bitch would reek to high hell! Probably get an STD to boot!" Eric said.

"Well, we both eventually have to fuck one day bro; you know what they say, if you don't use it you lose it!"

"Nobody says that, dicknose!" Eric said.

"Well, they should then!" Dylan laughed.

They fell silent momentarily, after the adrenaline dump

of talkativeness subsided as quickly as it had appeared. They both felt on the cusp of something genuinely great. They could be the next Dahmer or Gacy, for Christ's sake, and the thought of that kind of infamy was delectable.

Eric got out of the car and went to the back and opened the trunk, looking through the bag of weaponry they had christened their implements of torture -- a loving homage to Albert Fish, a serial killer that they both felt was vastly under appreciated in the grand scheme of things.

Dylan bounded out and joined him, staring affectionately at the items they had brought.

Peter Scully had wanted brutality, and brutality was what he was going to get! In their eyes, they were already on the verge of becoming the next big thing on the dark web when it came to atrocious bloodshed.

"Damn bro, we are going to fuck these burdens of society up tonight, aren't we?" Dylan said.

"Hell, yeah dude! Whoever is unlucky enough to be in our murderous path is in for some unfathomable agony. My dick is already hard in anticipation!" Eric laughed.

"Bruh, same!" Dylan pointed to his crotch region. It was indeed hard as a rock.

"Gross, dude." Eric said.

"Whatever, just because you need Cialis, limp dick." Dylan giggled.

Eric playfully punched him in the arm for the spirited jab at his manhood.

"OWWW!" Dylan said dramatically, in mock pain. "You're going to leave a bruise now!"

Eric hefted the bag of destruction and closed the trunk as quietly as possible, in case anyone was close by. He didn't want anyone alerted to the danger they were presently in for. As he scanned his surroundings, he saw the glow of a roaring fire and heard the smattering of a conversation being held by at least two people, maybe more. He smiled to himself. It was like kismet, or the plot of a Hollywood action movie where everything was going the hero's way no matter what was thrown at him.

"Dude, do you hear that?" Eric asked.

They listened intently to the popping of hot coals, and two voices laughing heartily. One male and the other one was female.

Dylan grinned caustically. "Looks like we didn't have to go very far to get some potential victims!"

"Nope. And at least one is a chick, so we already know that we are going to get paid. Unless she is an elephant or something!" Eric said.

"Plus, it's a twofer, just as long as we fucking destroy the dude properly!" Dylan added.

"Fuck yeah, broski, let's go get our hands dirty!"

They crept towards the campfire in an almost orgasmic state of rapture. Shit was going to get very real and very messy in a moment.

***

The trio of newly formed acquaintances sat cozily by the roaring fire, enjoying their bowls of chili and some stimulating conversation. The night, though chilly and brisk was beautiful. A bevy of stars shone brightly down upon them.

It felt to Daisy that, somehow, everything was going to be all right for her and Hazel. Tomorrow was another day, and she knew she could turn things around in her life. She watched Sid as he tended the fire by applying more wood to the hungry flames. How could someone that had almost nothing offer so much? How could a total stranger be more accommodating than her own wretched mother?

"Besides being my guardian angel, what is your story Sid? How'd you end up on the streets?"

"Well , it's not much of an original story, I'm afraid. Pretty cliché. After 'Nam ... I guess you could say I was never quite right. Mentally, I mean. I had to do a lot of terrible things there. Things my own government commanded of me, and my peers. They fed us tons of dope to keep us nice and high, so we couldn't think much about what we were doing. It was a losing battle, though. Us jarheads could never get on top of the Viet Cong. It felt like every ten we killed, another fifty would sprout up, like a bunch of goddamned dandelions! I watched men, women and even children die like they were little more than deer. I saw women and kids routinely raped and then get a bullet to the brain after. I witnessed my best friend get blown up right in front of me and I had to shower his brain and skull fragments out of my hair and even from inside my ears."

"Oh my God, that is terrible! What happened after you got back?" Daisy asked.

"The whole town threw me a big welcome home party. Everyone, at first, was happy I was home. My folks, my girl, my job. I tried to go back to my old, boring life, but my mind wouldn't let me. It was like I was still in the war, watching all that death and destruction all over again! I had nightmares constantly, could barely sleep at night. Any loud or abrupt noise caused me to piss myself and take cover. I eventually lost my job because the factory was just too loud, and every little thing would trigger me into hysterics. Eventually my girl left me as well. I moved back in with my parents, but eventually they grew tired of the 'new me' too. So, I moved out, so I wouldn't be a burden to anyone, and I became homeless, and I've been on the streets ever since."

"I'm so sorry to hear that, Sid. If we had a home, you could live with us!" Hazel said hopefully.

Daisy watched as Sid's face crumpled from the sweet words of her young daughter. Tears flowed from his bloodshot eyes and he furiously pawed them away with a crumpled piece of Kleenex. After he composed himself, Sid addressed Hazel.

"You are just a total sweetheart, young lady. It would be an honor to live with you and your mom. I haven't had a family to call my own in a long time."

"We can be your family!" Hazel offered.

"I agree!" Daisy chimed in.

"Well, I feel like I just won the lotto. You know it's

funny how life works sometimes. Even after all my years on this planet, I still can be surprised!"

Daisy was fixing to respond, until she saw two teen boys emerging from the shadows, grinning from ear to ear. One of them carried a tattered, bulging gym bag.

Sid must have seen her smile vanish, because he whirled around to see what was wrong. One look at their lecherous faces, and Sid must have known they were definitely bad news. He quickly sprang to his feet and grabbed Hazel protectively.

"Spot's taken boys; I would suggest you look elsewhere to camp," Sid said aggressively.

Daisy was shocked by the almost seamless way Sid's voice had gone from tender to strident in a heartbeat. This must be the voice he had used on the battlefield. Strong, forceful, and commanding, it was the voice of a man that took no prisoners. His boldness emboldened hers, causing Daisy to get up and stand next to Sid.

"Yeah, guys, we were here first, so you two will need to move on."

"Yeah, kick rocks!" Hazel said, surprising everyone.

***

Eric stared at his three potential victims with a look of mirth etched across his face. *They're so dead, they don't even know it yet; it's kind of cute*, he thought to himself.

"Whoa, little girl, didn't your cunt of a mother teach you any manners?" he said. "And I know this flea-ridden fucking stew bum didn't teach you any either; he looks like a wildebeest."

"Yeah, you should definitely be showing us some respect; you're going to regret your shit-talk." Dylan chimed in.

Both sides glared at one another as if they were amid a wild west shoot-out, neither side budging momentarily.

It was Dylan who struck first. He rushed at the woman, grabbing her pregnant body roughly and wrestling her to the ground, causing the old man to loosen his grip on the little girl, which was the plan all along.

Eric quickly dropped his satchel and unzipped it, digging through its contents until he found what he was searching for. A heavy-duty clawhammer. He grasped the handle in a death grip and stridently marched towards the frazzled man while he was focused on Dylan and the woman wrestling in the dirt.

The old man must have sensed a presence behind him, as he angrily whirled around to face Eric. The minute he did so, the claw part of the hammer crashed into his left cheek, embedding itself deep inside the meaty flesh with a wet, sucking sound. His eyes opened cartoonishly wide in a mixture of pain and shock. He gaped as Eric yanked down on the hammer, ripping his cheek out in the process.

The old man howled in agony and danced around like he was standing on a bed of hot coals. While all eyes were on the flailing, hemorrhaging man. Eric repositioned the hammer and struck again, this time directly into his forehead with a sickening crunching sound. Skin split apart from the hellacious blow, sending a river of blood running down the grizzled man's face.

Eric watched in awe as the man's eyes rolled back into his head and he toppled, heavily landing on his back. Then Eric was on top of him, pinning his arms. He relished the sight of the old man's blood bubbling down his face, making a pleasant, babbling brook sound as the crimson flowed unperturbed.

His next blow smashed into the old man's other cheek, the sound of his bone fracturing into multiple pieces breaking up the shocked silence of the stunned audience. Dylan grinned in approval, drinking in the chaotic madness like an intoxicating drug. Eric got face to face with the man, their noses almost touching, as he listened to the labored, waterlogged gurgling of his labored breathing. It sounded like he was drowning from the sheer amount of blood pouring from his head wounds.

Eric once again swung the hammer, this time crashing the head of the tool into the man's mouth and detonating the front teeth from his gums. Setting the hammer down beside him, he reached into his bag of hellish implements to out a Phillips head screwdriver with his blood caked hand.

In the blink of an eye, Eric began punching into his victim's abdomen with the makeshift weapon. Again, and again, he stabbed the point of the screwdriver into the man's blubbery, yielding guts, sending the cold steel deep inside of his ravaged body. Obvious, gurgling sounds of agony emitted from his broken jaw. Eric kept stabbing, a feral, Hyena-like screeching sound radiated from him.

Dylan hooted in appreciation of the savagery on full display in the light of the fire light. "Yeah buddy! Fuck that piece of shit up, man!"

"Stop hurting Sid, mister!" the little girl cried.

The pregnant woman only looked on in shocked terror, as the atrocity played out like some kind of home movie from hell. Despite being held down by Dylan, she seemed rooted in place, as if she'd never in her life witnessed such barbarism.

Eric shot the little girl a black glare, causing the child to flinch back in terror, plopping heavily onto the wood stump where she had been sitting when everything was still okay. Her young mind probably couldn't fully comprehend what was truly happening. She had to know that the nice man -- Sid, she'd called him -- was being hurt; she was not a complete baby. But the full extent of the brutality must have been lost on her underdeveloped mind.

"I'll deal with you in a jiffy, kiddo," Eric said. An idea on how he wanted to kill her plopped into his poisoned brain, and it delighted him. "Just sit back and enjoy the show!"

He began stabbing the gore-flecked screwdriver blade deep into Sid's whisker-covered, scrawny neck, the point breaking through repeatedly. like a piercer's needle. The continuous puncture wound massacre was putting more holes into Sid than an Afghan blanket.

The old man spasmed and jerked as his violated and

abused body began to shut down from all the destruction being heaped onto it. Bloody snot bubbles swelled from his nostrils. They exploded with Sid's last, frail breath, spraying a fine mist of pink spray and bloody boogers into the cool night air.

Eric gazed down at the decimated corpse of the homeless man, regarding his handiwork with prideful awe. Juice, blood, and gore oozed slowly out of various puncture wounds, collecting in copious amounts. only to be absorbed by the dirt. Then he looked at the girl, assessing her lithe, minuscule frame appreciatively. It was going to be a real joy butchering this little cutie. He had just the tool for it too!

But first, he had to get her undressed, so the GoPro could film everything he was about to do in all its 4K glory.

"Come here to your Uncle Eric; I want to show you something."

She remained at the tree stump, stridently shaking her head.

"You're not my uncle, you're a bad man! You killed Sid, and he was good!"

"You're testing me kiddo. Trust me, you don't want to see me angry!"

She stood her ground still, crossing her arms with a huff and only glared at Eric. Eric, having had enough of her petulance, lunged at her and grabbed her by one delicate arm, breaking it in the process,

"OWWWWWW!!! YOU HURT MY ARM!!!!!" she

wailed.

At that, the woman couldn't take it any longer. With an aggression only a mother could muster, she wrestled free from Dylan's grasp and ran towards Eric, only to have her face met by Eric's size 15 Nike shoe.

The force of his kick sent her skittering backwards crazily before falling hard onto her rump. Dylan quickly grabbed her so she couldn't try and fight back again. Eric was enraged by her act of rebellion, but he would show her what happened to dissenters. He pulled the girl against him, whipped out his pocketknife, and hacked off her ear.

He was surprised with the ease with which the knife sliced through the helix and lobule. Only a thin stream of blood trickled from the newly made orifice in the little girl's head. She moaned and gobbled in pain, but was unable to break free from his iron-clad grip. He sneered at the woman, who was bawling at the pain her daughter was having to endure.

Eric brought the severed ear up to his mouth and began to speak into it.

"Your hearing isn't too good, bitch; I said be cool, or your kid pays the consequences for your misbehavior. Here, keep this with you so you can remember next time!"

He threw the appendage at the woman, hitting her in the cheek with it. It left a smattering of blood where it had struck her before falling to the ground noiselessly. Then he began yanking off the little girl's garments in a frenzy, until she was nude, her face scarlet, trying to cover her nonexistent breasts and her tiny vagina. She shivered in the moonlight, tears slowly tracked down her face as she cried silently.

"Relax, bitch, I'm not going to rape you. This is our first video; me and my boy are only interested in murder for now. Next time, we'll fuck a little brat senseless."

"Yeah, kid, today's your lucky day, you get to die a virgin!" Dylan laughed.

Eric lifted her into the air and flung her down as hard as he could, knocking the wind out of her. As she thrashed around on the ground, fighting desperately to regain her breath, he dug into his gym bag and acquired a hacksaw.

***

Daisy stared in abject horror at the tool. Everything felt so surreal, like a bad dream you can't wake up from. She kept expecting to snap out of it and wake up in her bed sweating profusely from this realistic nightmare.

But she wasn't asleep, and this was no dream, it was real and there was no escaping this. The monstrous boy - Eric - got on one knee and began sawing through Hazel's shin, the rusted teeth of the hacksaw chewing through tender meat. Blood spurted from the newly made wound. The thin, fragile skin opened like a blooming flower, exposing the fat and tendons beneath.

As Hazel howled in torment, Eric grinned, seeming intoxicated by her misery, and continued to saw into her leg until he had severed it completely. He looked almost shocked by the profuse crimson spilling forth. As if he didn't want her to bleed out, so he could prolong her suffering, he grabbed a piece wood from the fire and scorched the ragged flesh with the flames, and sealed off the blood's only exit. Steam billowed from the charred stump.

"AAAAAAAAAARRRRRRRRRGGGGGGHHHHHHHH!!!!!!!" Hazel screamed.

"Cry bitch, cry!" Eric screamed back, into the girl's plum-colored face.

"Oh man, this is getting me horny! How about you, mom? Is your pussy getting wet or what? Want to lick your little girl's blackened stump?" The other one, the one pinning Daisy, cackled.

Inhuman rage intermingled with madness blanket her psyche. She screamed and bucked against his grasp but no matter what, she couldn't get loose from the nefarious teenager.

"Hazel, baby, Momma loves you! I am so sorry this is happening!!!"

"Momma!" Hazel moaned drunkenly.

Eric began to cut again, the blood less pronounced as the saw's rusty teeth ate through her carpals, severing her hand from her gory wrist. Chuckling, he tossed the little hand behind him into the fire, then cauterized the stump again, to prolong his fun.

"Dude, we're going to be so rich from this!" his partner announced. "Cha-Ching, motherfucker!"

"This is about *money*?" Daisy asked, aghast.

"Duh, skank; everything in this world is about money!"

Eric crowed. "Crazy motherfuckers will pay top dollar for gnarly snuff flicks, so they can sell it to a bunch of rich ass voyeurs who revel in the destruction of women and children while they jerk off. Looks like you are guilty of going to the wrong place at the wrong time. Guess you dumb twats should have stayed home tonight!"

Daisy cried uncontrollably, thinking of the people that were truly at fault. Jesus and her mother had done this! Inadvertently, yes, but make no mistake about it, they were just as much to blame for her and Hazel's impending deaths as these two American psychos, if not more so.

***

Eric looked down at the pale, nude, bloodied child with absolutely no compassion whatsoever. She was the equivalent of shit stuck to the bottom of his shoe. He cut off the fingers of her remaining hand and deposited the detached digits one by one into her underdeveloped sex. It wasn't an easy task; not only was Hazel incredibly tight, but she was bone dry as well. With some effort, he finally got them all stuffed deep inside her.

By now, the girl hardly flinched from each new atrocity performed on her. Still, she hadn't died yet. Eric thought she might last for one more mutilation.

He brought out his trusty pocketknife and carved a slit down her torso, from sternum to pubis, opening her abdominal cavity like he was finding his favorite passage in a well-loved book. Then, with a trowel from his bag, he went to the fire, scooped up a heap of glowing embers, and deposited them into her gaping gut.

The sound of coals hissing vehemently as they struck her wet intestines was music to his ears. The girl squealed in hurt and pain, eyes bugging out of her tiny, sweat-drenched head. As she weakly called out for her mother once more, Eric, grinning, scooped another load and crammed the burning coals into her mouth, expanding her cheeks like a chipmunk foraging nuts.

That was that; it was over. Smoke funneled out of the dead child's mouth like an overstuffed ashtray.

The mother looked comatose as Eric got back up on his feet. Drool slowly plummeted from her slack lips, landing on her bulbous, pregnant belly.

This had been fun and all, but killing people was arduous work! Eric wanted nothing more than to finish this slag off, grab something to eat, go home, shower, and smoke a blunt before hitting the hay.

He went over to her and punched her solidly on the chin. It wasn't like in the movies, though. Punching someone hurt your hand as well.

Blood from the solid strike joined the drool, but she otherwise didn't react. Eric stared at her coldly while Dylan kept a firm grip on her, in case she was playing possum.

"Hey. I'm not through with you bitch. Snap out of your stupor, cunt!"

"My baby," she moaned, mumbling it over and over "My baby. My baby. My beautiful, sweet girl. Momma's sorry. I love you. I'm so sorry."

It seemed like the bitch had gone off the deep end. Eric supposed seeing your little girl turned into human hamburger might do that to a person.

"Dylan, get this whore on the ground and undress her for me, would you?"

"Fuck yeah, brother, let's see what this pregnant slut looks like naked!"

Dylan flung the woman onto the hard ground so hard that she bounced from the impact. He tore off all her clothing, every stitch. Her pallid, nude form looked almost luminescent in the glow of the moonlight.

Eric's cock became rigid with delight as he thought of fucking her AND mutilating her in the process. He shed his jeans and boxer briefs as quickly as possible, allowing his cock to pop out into the chilly night air. Dropping to his knees, he spread her legs painfully wide. She bleated and began to cry again.

How much a person could cry before they ran out of tears? This bulbous broad had an unlimited supply.

He grasped his rigid penis and began slapping the head of his cock against her clitoris, then worked the length of his prick inside the folds of her vagina just like he had seen in the pornos, but no matter how much he tried stimulating her cunt, it wouldn't moisten.

"I think this bitch's pussy is broke or something!" Eric lamented.

"How come?" Dylan asked.

"Cuz it isn't getting wet, that's why!"

"Well, shit, bro, I read somewhere that blood is the best lube; just use that!" Dylan said.

"Good thinking dude!" Eric said.

Grabbing his pocketknife, he tried to figure out the cruelest way to draw blood from her. She was still yammering incessantly about her dumb kid, and it was getting on his last nerve. Killing his vibe, if he was being honest. He seized one of her enormous breasts, pinching the nipple, yanking it nice and taut. With a flick of the glade, he severed nipple and areola, then did the same thing to the other breast.

As she began bucking and gibbering like a mad woman, Eric shoved the severed titty meat deep down into her gullet, shocking her first, then choking her on her own mangled mammary meat.

"Shut the fuck up, sow; I'm trying to fuck this busted ass pussy of yours!" Eric hissed.

He cupped a hand to her damaged breasts, collecting the piping hot blood into his palm like a ladle. He then slathered her cunt with her ruby fluid, and coated his cock with it for good measure. This time, he sank balls deep into her gory slit with no problem at all. His hips pumped him in and out of her sloppy box. He sliced some long gashes into her inner thighs as he raped her, more blood cascading down into her cunny. Eric laughed with malicious glee.

"It's raining blood from a lacerated sky!" Dylan sang.

"Bro, are you quoting Slayer lyrics as I pork this pregnant skank?" Eric smirked.

"Seemed appropriate, broski!"

Eric continued to pummel her pussy and slice deep grooves into her tender, yielding flesh. He carved crude hearts into her skin, like one might find on the bark of an old tree. He even flayed long strips from her quadricep, just for the hell of it. Eric took one of the strips and popped it into his mouth like a potato chip, and thought it tasted mighty fine!

"Dude did you just cannibalize this pregnant bitch?" Dylan asked, amazed.

"Tasted just like chicken homie!"

"That's some gnarly shit!" Dylan said.

"You going to have a turn, or what?" Eric asked.

"And get your sloppy seconds?"

"This pussy is mine; you should skull fuck her!"

"Give me your knife so I can cut her eyeball out, then!"

"Quit being a pussy and dig that shit out with your bare hands, pussy!" Eric sneered.

"Fine!" Dylan retorted.

Dylan peered into the woman's tear-ridden peepers. They rolled around mindlessly, no doubt from the beating her pussy was taking from Eric's young, vigorous cock. The lights may have been on, but no one was home.

After steeling himself for a moment, Dylan plunged his thumb and pointer finger into her eye socket and quickly yanked the baby blue orb out of its housing. A deluge of icky fluid and blood blurted out, trundling down her cheek. Dylan was preparing to toss her eyeball over his shoulder until Eric called out.

"If you throw that away, so help me God, I'll whoop

your ass! Give it to me fucker!"

Dylan meekly handed over the grisly goods.

"Now skull fuck that bitch!" Eric commanded.

Dylan did exactly as Eric had said. He quickly dropped his pants and jabbed his pecker into Daisy's eyeless socket. He sunk into its gooey, warm confines and audibly moaned from the exquisite feeling. He quickly started pumping in and out of her noggin with wild abandon.

"Now that's what I call getting head!" Eric laughed.

Looking at the eye in the palm of his hand, a brilliance struck Eric. He pulled his blood-coated dong out of her cunt with an audible pop, tucked the eyeball into its folds, then slowly pushed it in with his cock head until he had buried it deep down into the confines of her snatch.

"Now you can get a look about what you are all about whore!" Eric spat.

Under the light of the moon, the macabre scene of debauchery went on as they both had at it with an almost animalistic fury, disregarding the human fleshlight like she wasn't even a human being anymore. She had become merely an object. A tool for their pleasure, nothing more, nothing less.

Eric came first, filling her cunt with his semen, grunting like a pig as he did so. Dylan came not long after, shuddering with ecstasy, shooting ropes of steaming jism deep inside of her skull,

Pricks slicked with slimy gruel and viscera, they got up and loomed over the incoherent woman, smiling with obvious pride from the sadism heaped upon her.

"I got one more idea, dude." Eric said.

"What's that man?" Dylan asked.

"Just watch!"

Eric bent over the swollen belly and sliced it open with his trusty pocketknife. After he was satisfied with the size of the cut, he began peeling apart membranes and parting the steaming tissue until he reached her uterus. He carefully cut into it and dug around with both hands, slopping himself in blood and amniotic fluid to his elbows before he secured hold of the fetus.

If the woman wasn't dead already, she was by the time he'd reeled the baby out of her like a fish on a line. Nearly full-term, it screeched and cried as soon as it felt the chilly night air bristling its young, delicate flesh.

Eric carried the slippery mass, placenta and all, over to an old patch of asphalt, where there'd once been a parking lot by the edge of the woods.

"Come here and hold onto this thing, dammit!" he told Dylan.

Dylan did, holding the baby pressed to the asphalt, its little head resting against the curb.

The baby loudly objected the only way it could, with ear-piercing squeals of contempt. Eric raised his leg high above the squawking baby's skull before pistoning his heel into its skull as hard as he could muster.

The results were horrific. The child's head burst apart like a ripe, juicy melon, vomiting its brain matter like a drunk frat boy at a kegger. Skull fragments skittered across the asphalt like a shattered beer bottle.

"NEWBORN BABY CURB STOMP MOTHER FUCKER!!!!!" Eric bellowed with glee, then howled at the moon.

"Broski, we are going to be so rich! I bet no one has filmed anything more heinous!"

"Yeah, I think we surpassed a new level of brutality!"

"I want to watch me skull fuck this skank again!" Dylan tugged his GoPro headband off, fiddled with it, and then suddenly groaned.

"What's up, can't stand the gore, pussy?" Eric teased.

"Uh, broski, I, uh, don't know how to exactly say this…"

"Just spit it out already, cut the suspense shit!"

"I forgot to hit record…"

"Fuck, man, did you eat a brain tumor for breakfast or something? Thank God I'm wearing mine; we still got most of it!"

But, when he took his off, he found himself gawking at it like some new species of exotic animal. He felt his face take on the hue of a brick as he stared unbelievingly at his GoPro.

His turned off GoPro.

Somehow, in the excitement for the night's depravity, they had *both* forgotten to power on their devices? They had just created the most brutal snuff flick ever made, and they had no footage to show for it? Worse than that, they would receive no money for their hard work!

They looked at one another for an awfully long time before both bursting out in gales of laughter, clutching each other as tears of unadulterated amusement plummeted from their eyes. tittering uproariously from their idiocy.

"I guess we know what we're doing tomorrow night, huh, bro?" Dylan said.

"Re-do!" Eric laughed.

Exchanging good-natured claps on the back, then gathered up their supplies to make the long trek back to Eric's car. Even though they had royally fucked up, it had been a fun night regardless.

As they walked, Eric remembered what his English teacher, Mr. Thompson, always said in class. *If at first you don't succeed, try, try again.*

He was right. Eric decided not to dwell on the past, and instead look forward. He thought about the twin fourteen-year-old girls that lived next door to him, and felt arousal immediately surge to his grimy, gory dick.

That would make a better video than some trashy, pregnant cow any day. He hoped they were still pure, so he could devirginize them with his bayonet, maybe cut off their young, firm tits and bathe in their adolescent blood. Then he wondered what their severed heads would look like on a stick.

By the end of tomorrow night, he would have his answer.

KIDNEY STONES:
An American delicacy

By Stuart Bray

I was only thirteen when I tried my first taste of kidney stones from a public toilet in the park.

I can still hear my mother, berating the hell out of me, when she caught her only son on his knees, picking little pebbles from a dirty white toilet bowl.

"What in the fuck is wrong with you?!"

I shrugged as my mouth still watered profusely.

Why did the taste have to fade away? What could I eat that tasted anything like these little mushy rocks? I had tried everything from frozen peas to black-eyed peas; nothing came close. I wish I had been able to follow the man out of the toilet, follow him to his house, I could sneak in at night and check his personal bowl.

"These motherfuckers have to pass!"

I'd heard his cries of pain in the stall next to mine on that hot summer day. My mother had taken me out to the park, saying she needed the fresh air, and for me not to wander off. I had to take a serious shit after eating a big bowl of cabbage soup last night, so I ran into the little restroom hut. I just barely made it to the last of three stalls lined up on the left side of the restroom.

"Jesus!" I called out, as my pants hit the floor and the

watery shit sprayed from my purple starburst.

I'd luckily made it to the seat. I did not, however have time to wipe it off before I planted my bare ass. I cringed at the thought of sitting on someone else's hot piss-drops.

A bead of sweat rolled down the tip of my nose; it was hotter than the broom closet of a Tijuana whorehouse. I looked to my right, where there should have been a toilet paper dispenser. There wasn't one to be seen, only a non-painted-in square where one once hung.

"Shit!" I said, anxiously looking around for something to wipe my melted ass crack with. I thought about using my shirt; what other option did I have?

"Need some TP, guy?"

A voice with a thick Boston accent was followed by a hand reaching under the stall wall, holding a crinkled wad of toilet paper.

"Um, yeah, thanks." I took the paper, knowing it wasn't enough to clean the train wreck that had just shot from my turd cutter.

I would have to make do; I wasn't about to ask this stranger for more. The small wad went far enough up my Chinese oil well to make me moan under my breath, but didn't clean it the way I had hoped.

"Gotta pass these stones; shit's brought me to my fuckin knees."

I glanced at the wall as I pulled up my pants; the guy grunted and hissed like a woman giving birth to a mongoloid. Then I checked to see the damage I had caused; it was kind of a hobby of mine. I shook my head in amazement at the brown gravy colored water with little chunks of meatballs floating around like bobbers. How much of that juice was still caked to my ass? Would my mom smell it on the way back home?

"Hurts worse than pissing out fuckin razor blades, these fuckin stones."

I stood there for a moment, hoping the man hadn't heard me getting up, not wanting to come off like some weirdo listening in on his personal business. Stones? I wondered how big they were. What did they look like in the toilet water?

The restroom lights above the sinks flickered in the heat. I was so sweaty that a puddle had begun to form around my sandals. The putrid smells stayed hovering under my nostrils. I wasn't sure how much longer I could stand here; even my unflushed shit had started to change shapes.

"God fucking damn!"

The man cried out so loud that I nearly had to sit down again. "Are you alright?" I asked, starting to feel slightly concerned for his wellbeing.

He was silent for a moment before clearing his throat.

"You sound like a kid; no kid should be hearin all this. Suck up your doody and hit the bricks, don't need ya havin nightmares."

I didn't want to leave, I wanted to see these stones he talked about. "I'm not quite finished yet. I ate something pretty ripe last night, might be awhile."

"You ain't lyin kid; smells like a dead whore in a dumpster

over there." The man stopped for a moment, as if remembering he was still sharing the restroom with a child. *"I mean- shit, Sorry kid."*

"It's alright; my mom and dad cuss a bunch. I'm used to it."

The man went to respond, but was cut short by another burst of agonizing groans.

"Don't know how much longer I can take this."

I felt awful for the man in the next stall, and glad I had never known pain like that in my life.

Finally, after a few more minutes of the man groaning, he stood up from the toilet. He had on big brown work boots and faded blue jeans; he must have worked in construction. He pulled up his jeans, then took a big breath before turning around to face the toilet bowl.

"Of course, the fuckin handle is busted. Well, I ain't no plumber, so fuck it. Take it easy, kid; good luck with your shit."

My heart jumped for joy, knowing that I would be able to see the stones he had pissed out. My mind raced, thinking about the shapes and colors they must be. I had never been so intrigued about something in my entire life.

The man stumbled out of the restroom. He moaned and groaned all the way around the corner until I couldn't hear him anymore. Without hesitation, I burst from my bathroom stall, quickly entering the other.

"Wow!" I said, looking down into the now pink toilet water. I assumed that some blood must have come along for the journey from the man's penis when he released the beauties that lay before me.

They weren't brown, like I had pictured in my mind, and not nearly as big. They looked like dark grey pebbles that someone had casually dropped into a public toilet.

"For a good suckin, call mama fuckin," I read aloud from the crude art mostly scratched in or written in permanent markers on the tan colored walls.

The cracked tile beneath my feet was slightly slick with drying up piss. I ignored it and dropped to my knees anyways. I reached my hand into the warm water, the smell of urine becoming more overwhelming the lower I went.

"Mikey? Are you in there?"

I jumped at the sound of my mother's voice, calling out to me from outside the restroom.

"Um, yeah, I'll be out in just a second." I turned back to the bowl, my mouth watering like a starving Ethiopian.

I pinched one of the stones in between my fingertips. It was hard, like an uncooked lima bean.

"You've been in there for a long time, Mikey. You need to hurry up because they are about to start work on that new road. I don't want to be stuck in traffic."

I tried to block her out so that I could focus on the task at hand. I brought the little gray stone out of the bowl. Piss and blood dripped from my fingers, almost drying instantly from the heat.

The stone was so fascinating that I almost didn't want to eat it, but I closed my eyes and shoved it in my mouth anyways.

At that very moment, my world changed.

"Wow, that is..." I chewed the little stone fiercely as it broke apart into tiny pieces that slid between my cheek and jaw, the texture almost trumping the incomparable deliciousness.

I immediately grabbed another, then another. The little pile they had formed into was now floating around in the water like a spooked school of fish. At this point, I was ingesting as much contaminated water as I was these tasty little treats.

"Mikey!?"

I spun around so fast that I nearly fell against the rim of the toilet.

My mother stood before me in utter disbelief, her face in a state of shock and disgust.

"What in the fuck are you doing? Are you eating from a fucking toilet?!"

"I wanted to see what they tasted like," was all I could say with my mouth still full of mushy delight.

Before I could think another thought, my mother grabbed the back of my shirt, dragging me away from my meal, and out of the restroom.

She screamed and shouted jumbled outrage as she shoved me with all her might into the backseat of her station wagon. Everyone in earshot rubbernecked to see what was happening. I slouched down in the seat as I watched my mother walk angrily around the front of the car, shaking her head in embarrassment.

During the awkward drive back home, we passed a group of construction workers unloading their truck on the side of the road, I wondered which one of them cooked up the heaven I could still taste on my tongue.

"*You ate some pretty weird things when you were little,*" my mother said, still shaking her head as we pulled to the curb next to the townhouse I had spent my entire childhood in. "*Nothing like this, though.*"

"I'm sorry Ma," I mumbled.

She grabbed her purse and opened the driver's side door. "*You wait until your father hears about this.*"

My stomach tightened and my mouth went dry; the thought of my father's face after my mother told him about my little snack today was enough to instill immediate fear.

I found myself not wanting to get out of the car. I didn't want any more scrutiny from my mother, and sure as hell didn't want it from my father.

My mother stepped out of the car, then cried out in alarm as a dump truck full of gravel flew by on the narrow street.

"*Watch were you're going, you prick!*"

My mother hated living in the city; she always said there wasn't room to breathe. She bent and looked at me through the window, still sitting in the backseat.

"*You can't stay there forever, Mikey. Your father is going to be home soon, and he is going to wonder why you're hiding out in the station wagon.*"

It seemed like her tone was starting to calm; it wasn't nearly as hostile as it sounded a few moments ago. She forced a smile.

"*If you come inside and help me get the dishes put away, I won't tell your dad about ... the incident. It can be our little-"*

Right before my very eyes, my mother disappeared underneath another passing dump truck.

*

10 years later

Even after all these years, I can't close my eyes without seeing her body on the street.

"It's a hell of a thing son. I'm truly sorry."

The policeman had put his hand on my shoulder before walking off into the sea of flashing blue and red lights.

"Ma?" was all I could say, as my mother's body parts were being shoveled off the blacktop like piles of cow shit.

My father arrived home shortly after; you could only imagine the look on his face.

"Missy!"

He cried out, as he crumbled to the ground.

That was the first and last time I ever saw my father cry, before blowing his brains out with a pistol he bought off some crackhead behind our building.

"I haven't thought much about them recently," I said now. "Had my own shit going on."

My therapist nodded her head, scribbling something in her notebook, I always assumed she was just writing random shit that had nothing to do with what I was saying.

"What about your urge to consume kidney stones? Is that

still an issue?"

I hated when she brought that shit up, I should have never said a word about my little indiscretion, should've just kept Mom and Dad the primary topic.

"I haven't eaten any kidney stones in a long time," I lied straight through my teeth. "I'm done with all that."

I had been volunteering at the local hospital for almost three-years now, it was an all you could eat buffet.

"I really don't think these sessions are necessary after all these years," I added. "We talk about the same shit every week."

Dr. Leslie jotted something down again before looking back up at me; goddamn, she was smoking hot.

"You don't feel as if these sessions have helped you through dealing with all that trauma? Do you want to stop coming? Do you think you still need your medication?"

I shifted in my chair. I didn't want to stop taking my medication; it was the only thing that kept me from losing my shit completely. Plus, I still had hopes that I could bang Dr. Leslie.

"I just don't think they need to be a weekly thing anymore, that's all." I folded my hands in my lap, trying to focus on anything but those long tan legs that were crossed just a few feet in front of me.

"Do you want to lick my ass cheeks?"

I looked over at her with my left eyebrow raised high. "I'll do whatever you want me to do," I said with a cheeky smile, only for Dr. Leslie to squint through her glasses in confusion.

"*Excuse me?*"

Fuck, she hadn't actually asked me that. Now she'd really think I was crazy. "Um, nothing, sorry, just a little sleep deprived." I fumbled around with my words and shifted uncomfortably in my seat. What a fucking putz.

"*I'm going to recommend a higher dose of what you're already taking.*" She scribbled on her prescription pad before offering the most forced smile anyone had ever given me in my fucking life.

"Yeah, um, thanks."

As she leaned forward and handed me the little slip of thin paper, I tried my hardest to not look at her perfect tits that poked out slightly enough to wave hello.

"Look somewhere else!" the voice in my head shouted, but I evidently wasn't listening.

Before I could avert my pervy gaze, I was caught red-handed. Dr. Leslie learned back quickly, adjusting her top. Then she then checked her tiny wristwatch.

"*I'll see you next week.*"

As I walked out of the office building onto the busy sidewalk, I slapped myself in the forehead.

"Fucking creep!" I said. "You are a fucking idiot!"

I smacked my forehead once more as a few onlookers looked at me the way they looked at the crazy homeless guy down on Jericho Street who was always screaming in people's faces.

"Sorry." I said, nodding to the old couple that tutted at me.

I finally reached my crummy-ass third floor apartment,

half expecting my door frame to be shattered to pieces for the third time this month. "Kato!" I called, entering a shit hole that not even rats wouldn't even piss on.

My Chocolate Lab came running over to greet me.

I knelt to love on him. "Hey big guy!" I scratched his belly as he rolled over, his long tongue dangling from his mouth.

Suddenly, he yelped, jumping to his feet, and running off to hide behind the couch.

"We'll get them out soon, bud. They aren't big enough just yet; I know they hurt."

This was the third time in Kato's life that I had intentionally given him kidney stones. It got harder every time.

"You have to watch what you are feeding him. I feel like we see each other way too often for the same issue, cool it with the treats."

On previous visits, the uppity fucking vet stood there with his arms crossed, judging me like I was some piece of shit. I was sure this time around wouldn't be any different. The last two times I had taken Kato to the vet to have his kidney stones removed, I had asked to keep them.

"Why would anyone want to keep these?" the dick head vet would ask, in a condescending manner.

"It's my fucking dog, so it's my fucking business," I would say, snatching the red biohazard bag full of deliciousness.

I would get home and open the bag to hundreds of tiny little greyish stones; the smell alone made my mouth water. I would eat my fill, then store the leftovers in the freezer for later, while Kato moped around the apartment, still high on doggy painkillers.

"We'll go to the vet and get those taken out soon," I told him. "Daddy is so excited to see what you've got cooking up in there!"

I smiled as I threw him another doggy biscuit, before rummaging through the freezer, looking for any stones that had maybe fallen out of the previous bags. I knew there wasn't going to be anything, but it was worth checking.

I had given myself kidney stones a few years ago before moving into my apartment; it hadn't gone as well as I had hoped. I remember drinking soda and iced-tea every fucking day for like six-months straight, before finally feeling a sharp pain in my abdomen. I went to the hospital that night, only to find out I had appendicitis.

Afterwards, I had the bright idea of volunteering at the hospital. You wouldn't believe how many people came in with kidney stones, only to have a doctor tell them that they would pass on their own. Un-fucking believable. But I was there once when some old coot had to have a handful of stones surgically removed.

"Take these to the incinerator," the doctor ordered, as he handed me my soon to be *snack pack*.

I ran straight to the hospital basement, stopping at the bottom of the steps to open the bag and get a big whiff. "Goddamn!" I cried out as my mouth literally dripped with saliva. I scarfed them down so quickly, I nearly choked.

Fast forward back to present day, as I sulked in disappointment that I had zero stones to snack on.

I laid in bed that night with the thought of my shitty job dangling above my head like a black cloud of despair. I only volunteered at the hospital, so there was no money coming from any time spent there. My bill-paying job was being a tollbooth operator over on the east end bridge; shit was mind numbingly boring.But I was lucky to still have even that shitty job, considering one of my co-workers accidentally ate some kidney stones I had brought in a little sandwich baggy. I wasn't paying attention after placing the bag next to me on the desk, and the next thing I knew, Joe was gagging, spitting all over the inside of the tiny booth.

"What the hell are you doing?" I asked looking confused as all hell.

"I just grabbed a couple of the things you had on the desk! What the hell was that shit?!"

I grabbed the baggy and stuffed it into my pocket. "Beans my aunt sent me from Rhode Island. You don't like them, I take it?"

Joe looked at my funny, his face still red from all the gagging he had just suffered through.

"Those don't taste like any beans I ever had; shit must be fucking rotten!"

He picked up the little black trashcan we kept on the floor and spit in it until his mouth was as dry as a camel's ass-crack.

"Well, you shouldn't just grab food that doesn't belong

to you," I said, shaking my head in disapproval.

Fortunately, Joe didn't choke and die; it would've been tough to explain why there was a kidney stone lodged in his throat.

My alarm buzzed just as I finally had dozed off.

"Motherfucker." I mumbled to myself as I rubbed my eyes and rolled out of bed.

I walked towards the bathroom to take the best piss of the day, then noticed Kato lying at the foot of the bed.

"You alright, boy?"

Kato didn't respond as he usually did.

"Kato?" I asked as I sat down on the edge of the mattress. "Fuck."

His body was stiff, his eyes only slightly open, his floppy wet tongue bone dry.

"Fuck!" I cried out as I slid down on the floor.

I quickly called Joe and informed him as to what had happened, and that I wasn't going to be at work today.

"I don't have anyone to cover you, Mikey. I worked all goddamn night; I need your ass in here!"

I hung up the phone before he could get another word out.

I was totally devastated. Just the thought of all those perfectly good kidney stones going to waste ...

"Maybe I still have time!"

I slipped on my house shoes and scooped up Kato's body.

"Jesus fucking Christ, you're heavy!" I moaned as I descended the steps of my apartment building. I guess it had been my fault that Kato had put on so much weight; I had him living off cheap dog treats his entire life.

As I ran, I imagined that this was the same feeling a farmer would have in his gut if he lost all the crops he had spent so long growing, losing out on the big payoff. I hoped and prayed the stones were salvageable, I mean, why wouldn't they be? He'd only been dead for a few hours at most.

Have you ever been called up to the front of the classroom to solve a math problem on the chalkboard that you didn't have a fucking clue how to do? You have all those eyes on you, the room is quiet, you're praying for a fucking bell to ring or a nuke to hit the school? Well, that's how I felt running through downtown with a big dead dog in my arms.

By the time I reached the front door of the vet's office, I nearly collapsed from exhaustion. "I need help!" I called, in the middle of a crowded waiting room.

"What seems to be the problem?" The old lady receptionist stood up from her chair to get a better look at the situation.

"My dog, he died." I looked down at Kato, his face frozen with death. "I know you can't do much, but ... I need the doctor to take out his kidney stones."

The receptionist looked around the room at the other people, who also clearly thought I was batshit crazy.

"I don't understand. You're saying that the dog is dead, but you want its kidney stones removed? May I ask why you- um, why?"

My cold cheeks defrosted from the burning

embarrassment I now felt. "How about minding your business, bitch?" I stepped forward as the people in the waiting room started whispering amongst themselves. "All of you people can shut the fuck up, too!" I growled while still fixated on the receptionist. The room went silent. "Get me the fucking vet, or I'll take them out myself."

The petrified receptionist backed up slowly, nodding her head. After a few seconds, she returned with the dick head vet who had given me shit the last two times I was here.

"I hear there is some sort of problem with Kato?"

This motherfucker had to be in his twenties, some gas station owning dot head with a smug attitude.

"Kato has more kidney stones; I need them out before they start to go bad."

The doctor looked over at the receptionist, like she would have an answer.

"I'm not talking to her, Muhamad."

The vet looked back at me, obviously offended. *"Excuse me? For your information, I'm native American, you, racist prick."*

I stepped forward, my eyes burning with rage. "Cut this fucking dog open and get the fucking stones out. If you don't, your kids' native name will become *'bastard with no dad.'* Got me?"

His demeanor changed rather quickly as he stepped forward and took Kato from my arms.

"I want every one of them. And make it quick, I must stop by the hospital for a pick-up."

The vet nodded his stupid fucking head and went to the operating room.

He reappeared half an hour or so later, sliding off bloody latex gloves, and told me, *"Kato didn't have kidney stones."*

I had been sitting on my ass against the hallway wall; now I got up. "No kidney stones? What the fuck are you talking about?!" I grabbed the smug fuck by his lab coat. "Are you fucking lying? Why? Are you trying to keep them for yourself? That goddamn dog had all the symptoms it had the last two times I was here!"

"Kato had a tumor in his lower abdomen. It wasn't kidney stones causing the symptoms this time." The vet pulled loose and shoved me away, then adjusted his coat in frustration. *"You're a real piece of work, you know that?"*

"I want the tumor."

"What?!"

"I want the fucking tumor."

"You are a sick individual; you need serious help."

"You fish car keys out of animal's asses for a living; don't psychoanalyze me! Go get me the tumor. My dog, my property."

"I'll give it to you, but don't come back here ever again."

I walked out with a red biohazard bag in tow, wondering what a dog's tumor tasted like. I could fry this baby up, or see what it tasted like raw. I had tried cooking some kidney stones at one point, using some olive-oil and a pinch or two of garlic powder, but they'd tasted like fried shit.

Looking around to see if anyone was watching, I crept into a messy ally, ducked down behind a dumpster, and opened my bag. The smell wasn't as pleasant as the stones; the stones always had this tangy citrus smell mixed with morning breath, while this smelt like ... a bloody fucking tumor.

I did my best to ignore the smell as I reached into the bag. The tumor was soft on the outside, with a hardened center on the inside. It wasn't the easiest to hold onto; the blood and goo made it like holding a bar of soap in the shower. Gripping it in both hands, I closed my eyes as I quickly sank my teeth into it.

A thick, putrid gunk shot into my mouth and onto my chin. I chewed the tough meat for a few moments, while I tried to decide if it was worth eating.

"You gonna finish that?"

I looked up in surprise at an old homeless man who sat against the wall across from me.

"You scared the shit out of me! I didn't even see you there."

The man looked as if he hadn't showered in ages. His thick grey beard was knotted and full of debris.

"Sorry about that; people like me go un-noticed unless we're taking a big shit in the middle of the street. I'm real hungry. You wouldn't mind splitting that with a poor old bum like me, would you?"

I looked down at the tumor with a bite mark in the side of it. "You know what, go ahead, its all yours." I leaned forward as the man extended his hands excitedly.

"Thank you, thank you so much." He bit into it without hesitation.

"Enjoy." I said as I stood up and waved goodbye.

"Hey, buddy. I hate to ask, considering you gave me your food and all, but do you have a few bucks?"

I turned to look at the man, a lightbulb flickering on above my head. "You know, why don't you come back to my place? My dog just died, so I have a little extra room. You could stay with me for a bit."

The old man's face lit up like he had just found a full pack of cigarettes behind the dumpster.

"You mean it?"

He pushed himself up using the wall, his yellow teeth visible through his wide smile.

"Yeah, lets go." I smiled and gestured for the man to follow me.

"What is it that you do that you can just be letting someone like me stay at your place? You must be a very respected man, a real good man."

I put my arm around the bum as we walked down the sidewalk towards my apartment. "I'm kind of a farmer." I said with a huge grin.

A few days later I arrived home from work, dropping my coat on the floor next to my shoes.

"Come here buddy!" I called, patting my knees.

When my live-in companion didn't come running to me, I went into the other room to see what was keeping him.

"You poor little guy, you look tuckered out," I said with

my hands on my hips, leaning over my companion as he lay flat on his back in the middle of the floor. "I bet your poor kidneys are just killing you right now." I squatted to rub his dirty belly, and he moaned in pain.

"Please, mister."

I smiled as I rubbed his outreached hand against my face, then kissed it as I held onto it tightly.

"Let's get you to the bathroom," I said. "I have a feeling you have some little surprises waiting for me."

The Golden Cumpuss

By Stephen Cooper

The Golden Cumpuss was not where you went for a refreshing pint. It wasn't where you visited for a glass of wine, or to celebrate an event with a bottle of bubbly. It most definitely didn't serve Coke, Pepsi, Dr Pepper *(and all its ridiculous duplicates)*, Lemonade, Orangeade, Cherryade, or any other fucking 'ade.' And if you asked for a tall glass of water, well… don't ask for the fucking water; that's likely to end up getting you killed.

The Golden Cumpuss drinks menu catered to a different crowd. Not the 'after a tough day in the office' crowd, or 'a quick one with your mates before heading home to the two point four' crowd. The Golden Cumpuss served the elite, and therefore, the most fucking degenerate depraved sick assholes imaginable. The Golden Cumpuss was where you went to sample some of the finest urine in all the world. Down some grade-A puke. Gobble up a plate full of chunky shit with a side of lumpy snot and wash it down with your favourite blood. *They had every type from A to O.* And all of the above came in multiple different flavours and combinations.

Maybe you wanted some chink puke? Well, The Golden Cumpuss could cater for that. They had several fine Taiwanese imports working at the joint. They could barf right on to your plate with their gorgeous tits hanging in view so you could stare at those delicious dark nipples while they puked up the dinner you ordered in advance. *Or just whatever the sluts had eaten that day if you were visiting on a whim.* Who knows, maybe you'd get lucky and get a full lobster meal, or maybe you'd be eating regurgitated food-poisoned kebabs. *Both were as likely as each other.*

You might prefer Mexican? They had plenty of those too. You want nachos? Just get one of those dirty beaners to plonk themselves over your plate and let their brown eye drop the meal like it's fucking Deliveroo. Right to your door. Carlos or Maria don't mind; they were paid well, and loved serving up waterfalls of diarrheic shit directly from their overworked assholes. If you tipped them well they'd even let you lick their shitters clean before you started on the main course.

The same applied to Indian, Italian, Chinese, Vietnamese, whatever your needs. As long as it was coming out of a cunt, dick, asshole, mouth or vein, The Golden Cumpuss had you sorted. *That should be their fucking motto.* They may not have had the best record when it came to providing for vegans or allergies, but if you wanted some of that famous Kraut sausage, they could have Jurgen stick his meaty eleven-inch German cock down your throat and piss out some of Europe's finest export, or cum like a fucking stallion. *Only the finest man milk at this price point.*

Speaking of which, The Golden Cumpuss didn't give a fuck about half-fat, semi-skimmed, almond, soy, or any of that other hippie bollocks, but if you wanted milk, they had it. You could drink it directly from some large pregnant titties, or a recent young milf. *Or some saggy granny if that was your jam; they had a few of them out back they could dust off.* They could udder it out for you straight into a glass like the fucking ice-cream machine at McD's. *Except these bitches worked all the time.* Again, there was plenty of choice. As for the newborns that dropped from the pregnant mums' cunts, well, we'll get to that later.

Maybe you preferred the taste of nigger blood to boring whitey crimson? Not a fucking problem. Idia could cut one of her Nubian veins and top your glass right up without spilling a drop; the girl was a pro after working there for ten of her twenty years on the planet. She had some of the finest tasting spit as well, which was always a favourite amongst the regulars, *and was one of the cheaper drinks on the menu.* Not that money was an issue for any of the scumbags and uber-wealthy lowlifes that made regular trips to the Cumpuss. This place cost, and everyone with daddy's money, or an over-inflated pay check, was willing to pay.

Maybe it wasn't the colour of the boys and girls that was your priority? Maybe it was the size? Again, not an issue. Want a fat wop to take a pizza shit on your plate, just give The Golden Cumpuss a call in advance and you'll have a choice of several different Italians preparing your meal. Maybe you want some skinny tiny-pricked Jap to piss strawberries for you? Again, one quick phone-call earlier in the day, and Ren would stuff his malnourished slanty-eyed face full of those juicy red gems and either deliver it straight into your glass, or you gaping awaiting gob. *Customer's choice.* They had everything from midget gooks to inbred-trailer-trash-rednecks of all shapes and sizes. From quadriplegics to diabetics. The Golden Cumpuss prided itself on its diversity and inclusivity.

They had every type of cum and pussy juice available too, from the thick gloopy type to light little salad dressing sprays. You could have it as a drink or sauce for your meals. Cum and discharge was how The Golden Cumpuss originally started. Like some fancy cocktail bar, but instead of a Daiquiri or Manhattan, you could have Lance cum in some type O blood, or have Anastasia squirt directly into your mouth after eating watermelons all day. From there, things grew to the depraved flourishing cesspool that is now The Golden Cumpuss, and half the elite world was grateful for it. While the venue only held two-hundred max, it was always full and booked well in advance. Cooperate heads and business tycoons would book their quarterly business functions around the availability. You might get lucky with a cancellation and be able to do a walk-in, but it was extremely rare.

And all that was just the top part of the exclusive club, where you could drink the finest human waste while getting your dick wet and pussy licked with the exotic and high-quality low-class trash strippers and whores on offer.

Underneath, down in the VIP basement, was where the truly deplorable shit took place, and that's where Detective Royce Miller came into the equation.

Above, the girls and guys were looked after, and most worked there willingly, *albeit normally finding their way there due to shit circumstance.* They were paid well, and all had places on the company dime in an apartment block attached to the elite club. Their contracts stated that all their bodily fluids belonged to The Golden Cumpuss, so any pissing, shitting, puking or cumming outside of company hours needed to be bagged and brought in, but other than that, they were free to live their life outside of business hours. The hours were long and their diets controlled to suit the orders of the day, but if they wanted to go shopping, or catch a flick at the cinema, not a problem. Just remember to ziplock the popcorn poop.

But the ones below the upper level had zero privileges. They were brought to the club as part of a human trafficking scheme set up by Detective Miller in return for a discount on both floors, and a rather hefty payment on the side, as long as the human ingredients and playthings kept coming. The detective had been a regular at the club since the early days, and had built up quite the taste for everything that came out of Josie, *one of the younger girls to begin with who was now into her teenage years.*

He wanted her exclusively, but no dice, as she had another rich and influential admirer who always paid a lot for her services. Albeit different ones from Royce. The other admirer enjoyed licking the sweat from her beautiful young body, *something else offered on the menu.* Instead, Royce got a good discount to eat plenty of her piss and shit while fucking the gorgeous Asian before she cleaned up, which he then enjoyed watching while sipping on another mug full of her delicious clear pee or recent vomit.

In return for this discount, Detective Miller, though some rather nefarious contacts he had made on the force, supplied the club with a seemingly unlimited supply of meat, in the walking and talking form. Whether they were brought in from other countries, or caught trying to sneak in, or just picked up off the street, they all ended up in Royce's possession and were sold on to The Golden Cumpuss and their Gold-Card members' enjoyment.

The lower floors were where the steaks were made, and often eaten, with the poor bastards whose limbs were being munched on left watching themselves getting consumed while chained to the table. The chefs at the Cumpuss were God-damn geniuses when it came to keeping people alive while also fucking cooking them. It was rare for any of the meals to die while they watched their body parts being hungrily devoured by some smug rich cunt. Sometimes they'd even last a couple of meals, *if the original guest weren't super greedy, or didn't want a doggy bag.*

If you were one of the unfortunate souls to be sold to The Golden Cumpuss by the deplorable detective, then you were most likely going to end up in someone's gut, but that didn't mean it would be the first and only thing to happen. The place was a regular torture playground as well, with walls upon walls of weapons to use on the disposable life. Clients could cut them, hack them, eat their fucking eyeballs or ball balls, puncture their organs, dice their tits, slit their dicks any which way you please, cram nails up their assholes, whatever!

Pay the high price, they were yours to do as you pleased. Let your depraved sadistic fucked-up mind run wild. *If you could think it, you could do it!* And if you fucked them up too much and killed them to the point in which they couldn't even be presented as a reasonable already dead meal, they'd just end up in a stew with any other worthless parts kicking around.

… And if you wanted to nut in their corpses, of course you could; it almost went without saying. Nothing was off limits at The Golden Cumpuss, as long as you paid the premium and did it within the confines of the club… and this is where the story really begins.

*

"Fuck!" Josie gasped, double checking the third pregnancy test, which confirmed the dreaded news.

She already knew the result; it had become obvious as she began to show a little over the past few weeks, but she'd finally plucked up the courage to make one-hundred-percent sure, and got the answer she expected. She was up the duff.

All that extra morning sickness had made her popular these last few weeks with the puke slurpers, but at what cost? She didn't want a fucking baby! This was not the place to raise a child; hell, in a purely age sense, she was still considered by many to be a kid herself at sixteen.

Sure, she could make extra commission and tips with being milked, but fuck. A kid? Pregnant? How the hell had this even happened? She'd taken every precaution, other than the boring not fucking at all option, *which Detective Miller would definitely not approve off.* He loved fucking her young juicy cunt after she pissed on his face, almost as much as she did. Say what you want about the rancid barbarian; he sure fucked her good.

He'd probably want to eat the kid. That was what happened with all the others born in the club. Some of the other girls even purposefully got themselves pregnant so they could get extra work milking and have their kid eaten for a big one-off payday, but Josie wasn't sure about that. She didn't want the fucking thing, but, eaten? *That was a bit much.*

It wouldn't be her choice, though. Nothing would be for the next few months. They used to let women abort the mistakes, as foetuses were a delicacy on the menu, but raw or roasted newborn started fetching a much higher price, so the coat hanger was out less these days.

Now she'd have to stay inside until the kid was born. They treated the pregnant girls well *(which was another reason so many of the women got preggers)* and there was definitely a market for them within the walls of The Golden Cumpuss, but any chance to venture outside would be strictly prohibited. The moment they found out she was brewing a newborn, the bidding would start for the doomed little tyke. She cradled her stomach almost instinctively, knowing the kid would never live beyond its first day. While she was okay with that, she also couldn't help but feel a little sadness wash over her.

Josie had been part of the club since she was eight. At sixteen, she'd never envisioned a family of her own, only knowing the seedy walls of the depraved institution. She'd made friends here, and was popular, but didn't have any real connections. Royce treated her well *(it's all relative)*, and looked at her like she belonged to him. Her other admirer, *who she was never allowed to name,* lusted over her sweat, and watched out for her too, but neither were family. Not in the true sense, despite them both seeing themselves as a father figure to her.

The kid would be the first real family she'd ever know, and she might not even get to meet him before he was eaten alive. *Minimum.*

What a life.

*

The owners of The Golden Cumpuss were delighted to hear Josie was knocked up. They never forced the girls to get pregnant, as they believed a happy work place was a thriving workplace, but it always opened another bunch of avenues to exploit. They could add a little premium for pregnant pee, and milk the bitch.

The baby had already been pre-ordered by Josie's admirer without Royce knowing yet, *that was going to be a problem.* While pregnant, more people would would to drink her sick, and fuck her glowing ever-changing body. They knew Josie normally only fucked Royce, *more at his request than hers,* but pregnant fuck money was hard to turn down, and she was never officially exclusive to him, *nor would she ever be.*

They'd arranged for Josie to be waited on in her off hours, but she wasn't allowed to leave the complex until the baby was born. The admirer had offered more money than the club had ever received for a single meal, so Josie was top priority. They knew she had mixed feelings about the whole ordeal, but such was life at The Golden Cumpuss, and she was loyal. Never once had she complained about the life bestowed upon her, nor had she ever tried to run from it.

One thing was certain though; Royce was going to act like a fucking psycho when he found out.

*

"You fucking what?" the beefy no-nonsense browbeating detective shouted, upon hearing the news that he wouldn't get to eat his own spawn.

How fucking dare they? That was *his* kid, and as far as he was concerned, Josie was *his* girl. He'd been fucking that tight pussy since she was a child, and now they had the fucking nerve to tell him that some other asshole was going to get to eat her kid? His kid!!

Probably wouldn't even have the decency to fuck the little brat first. What a fucking waste! Royce was absolutely fuming.

A Golden Cumpuss employee tried to explain that their hands were tied, but Royce was having none of it. He'd supplied them with over half the livestock they had downstairs and they knew it. He should have been a fucking partner in the operation by now, not being passed over having first dibs on his own fucking sprog.

The employee kept his tone neutral, but wasn't getting anywhere. Despite having a couple of armed guards at the door, he knew someone higher up was going to have to explain to the pig-headed detective just how things worked around here.

Royce thought the way things worked around here was his way. That was how everything else in his life worked. The imposing cop was a fucking hurricane of violence and profanity and unyielding aggression. He was not to be crossed in any walk of life. He was one of the top detectives at the station because he always got results. If he couldn't find the perpetrator, then some innocent cunt would just have to go down for it, because no fucking way was he losing his one-hundred percent record due to some sneaky asshole thinking he could get away with shit. His bosses answered to him, as far as he was concerned. The bitch-ass pussy Commissioner was practically wrapped around his finger, and the rest of the men fell in line. And those that didn't, soon fucking did. Royce ruled the roost.

No criminal in the grimy streets of the city would dare talk back to him, or start shit in his presence. Anyone walking in his way better move aside, whether they'd done something wrong or not.

As for The Golden Cumpuss, he'd practically helped them build the place. He'd been there since the beginning, their most loyal customer, and top supplier by some fucking distance. The thought that they could even entertain the idea of fucking him over, *let alone actually doing it,* made his infected murky piss boil.

The nerve! The audacity! He'd a good mind to pull out his fucking hand-cannon and lay waste to every motherfucker in the the joint, and they knew he could. They knew not to fuck with him, yet... they were fucking with him. It's like they had a God-damn mother-cunting death-wish.

And that fucking whore, Josie! He couldn't be mad at her for long, as she was his girl after all, his little poop bunny, and the only person in his life he showed any softness towards whatsoever. He bet she didn't put up a fight, though. She knew this was his kid; wasn't no fucking way it was going to be anyone else's, including that faggoty sweat licker who didn't even have the balls to fuck his piss princess. But he knew she didn't protest. She always told him she loved him, but she was loyal to the club. Something he needed to change, because there was no way anyone else was eating his kid. HIS FUCKING KID!

Matthews, the executive Royce normally dealt with walked into the room with a smirk, clearly enjoying Royce's expletive uproar. They'd done good business together in the past, and shared the occasional asshole or pisshole, but for the most part couldn't be considered friends. Acquaintances, at best. Matthews was a company man, where as Royce was most definitely his own man. He answered only to himself, and always got what he wanted… until today.

"What appears to be the problem, detective?" Matthews asked, like he didn't fucking know.

"You know damn well what the problem is," Royce retorted with a roar in his voice and violence in his eyes. He was ready to tear this place apart.

"The baby?"

"The *fucking* baby," Royce confirmed.

"I'm afraid the child has already been pre-ordered. As far as we're concerned the case is closed." Matthew spoke like it was an everyday transaction to sell a kid to be eaten; *in the world of The Golden Cumpuss, that wasn't far from being true.*

"I wasn't even informed," Royce protested, taken aback by Matthew's matter-of-fact manner, although he tried his best not to show it.

"The offer we received far outweighed anything you could possibly offer; there was simply no point informing you. This was never going to be a bidding war," Matthews coldly told the irate detective.

Royce could tell he meant it, too. The offer must have been way into eight figures. Quite frankly, it was an obscene amount for one little baby, albeit one that was surely going to be delicious, and lord knows the spoilt admirer had the money.

"Anything I can possibly offer?" Royce shouted as his

ample neck muscles strained and the vein in his forehead bulged. "What I offer is a boat load of human scum for you to fucking cook and destroy every week. Without fail. For the last eight God-damn fucking years you smarmy cunt!"

"For which we compensate you generously," Matthews answered back without getting flustered or raising his voice.

It always pissed Royce off how damn calm everyone who worked here was despite the madness and cruelty of the business they were involved in. Why didn't they fucking bellow like the titans they were? He certainly did. What was the point in being so powerful if you're going to be quiet about it?

"That's my kid," Royce told the executive, with a look in his eye daring the cunt to deny him this.

"Congratulations," Matthews smiled without missing a beat.

That was it.

Royce lost the fucking plot and dove at him, swiping his bear paw at the tailor-made custom-suit-wearing prick's face. Matthews took a step back and shook his head in disappointment at the action as the armed guards stepped forward. Royce didn't give a fuck about them. He'd shoot them both dead before they even worked out what end of the gun to use. Then he'd fuck their mangled corpses before posting them back to their families… who he'd then fucking rape and kill too, and post them to whoever was next like some morbid chain mail.

Matthews gestured for calm.

"We have multiple girls pregnant at the moment, Detective Miller, and while all of their babies have already been purchased, I'm sure we can make a deal where you can have one, on the house. How's that for generosity?"

It was a good deal. Better than anything Royce had ever been offered before, and an act of kindness The Golden Cumpuss and Matthews rarely showed.

But none of those kids were his and Josie's baby. He had the money to buy a different kid to eat if he wanted; he was doing well with this side gig. No other detective on the planet, other than maybe some owned by the mafia, were making the cash he was, but he didn't want another baby. He wanted his. He wanted Josie's. He'd eaten ninety percent of the literal shit and piss coming out of her body since she was a child. He'd fucked her every week for the last eight years. He'd swallowed her spit and drunk her beautiful tasting blood. They swapped vomit and pus. Fuck, everyone of his birthdays since he'd known the girl, he'd gotten her to eat his birthday cake and shit out every last fucking piece of it into his mouth. He'd licked up the crumbs with his hungry faeces smeared gob.

Now he was expected to let some other cunt have their baby? No fucking chance.

Royce stormed out of the meeting without another word. He already knew what he was going to have to do if he ever wanted to have this baby. The fucking happy meal wasn't due for another five months, so he had time to arrange things. He was going to have to break Josie from The Golden Cumpuss's grasp, and get them both the fuck out of dodge.

Not an easy task for sure; in fact it was one that had never been successful before. But no one else who tried was Detective Royce fucking Miller.

*

The last person who did try vamoosing from The Golden Cumpuss was a girl named Alva.

An early twenties Swedish bombshell who'd ended up owing a lot of people a lot of money through some very questionable life choices, when it came to either taking a bullet and having her gorgeous corpse ravaged, or selling her services to The Golden Cumpuss, it wasn't much of a choice. She'd rather deal out the shit than take it.

Alva had become instantly popular at the club, offering something a little different coming from Scandinavia. There were plenty of other 'exotic' girls there, but most of the white girls were your typical English rose or valley girl slut types. Nothing with her outrageously defined bone structure. She was a goddess amongst the rich heartless playboy freaks, and treated like such, *in their own way*.

Men would book her weeks in advance to make sure they got to taste her Swedish meatball piss and shit, and fuck her perfect cleanly shaven pussy while she spat on them and chundered out the Räkmacka she'd eaten for lunch. She didn't like being a fucking waste dispenser, or a whore, but the only other option was death.

Until Simon came along.

Unlike the other guys who used and abused her, Simon loved her. Sure, he made her eat apple pie and devoured her scat when she shat in his mouth, but he was sweet to her. He always left a tip and had a laugh and joke with her. He'd ask her about her day, and her crazy life before working at The Golden Cumpuss. He wouldn't judge the bad choices she'd made. The copious amount of drugs. The insane cults. The murder. He recognised her for who she wanted to be, rather than who she'd been in the past.

And for that, she loved him dearly too.

The trouble with their love was that she spent six days a week spraying her juices down dudes' throats and vomiting shrimp into peoples' assholes, or whatever other crazy shit was on the menu. *Which was fucking everything.* She'd made more cash than she could ever have dreamt of, and had even paid her debts, but her contract with The Golden Cumpuss was for a life.

A life for a life, they'd told her. At the time, otherwise faced with the prospect of having a double barrel shotgun stuffed up her gash, it felt like a good deal. So she'd agreed. But now wanted out.

Both she and Simon weren't stupid, though. They knew The Golden Cumpuss wasn't to be crossed. He was an important up and comer in a major pharmaceutical company, so he understood the nature of the beast. And Alva had been told first hand what would happened should she try to run, or even miss a day of work. There was no such thing as sick days, *as that was on the menu too.*

But they loved each other. and would settle for a simple

life if it meant they could be together, so they had to try something ... no matter how foolish.

*

When they made their move, the person sent to track the naive lovebirds down was Detective Royce Miller. That's why he knew exactly what happened to those who crossed the company.

Alva and Simon had run on her day off. They left the city early in the day and made it across the country by the time anyone realised they were gone. They'd used cash the whole time, drove an unregistered car, changed their appearance, and kept out of view of any camera they could spot... yet they were still found by mid-afternoon the following day.

Little did Alva know the fuckers had put a tracking chip in her like some dumb mutt. *None of the girls knew they had these, but all did.*

The look on their faces when Royce turned up at their motel room was one he'd never forget. They couldn't fucking believe it, yet he hadn't taken a wrong turn the entire journey. In fact, the executives had known of their escape the moment they set off, as it was against policy to leave the city without warning. The fucking chip was sending back distress signals almost immediately, but the elite club decided to let them enjoy one night together before their punishment.

It was an act of kindness Royce wouldn't have afforded

them, but these people had their own way of doing business and it wasn't Royce's place to question it. As long as they paid him, it was all good.

He beat the holy hell out of them, and broke Simon's legs and arms before making him watch as he raped his girl over and over and over and over again. He'd been a fucking monster in the sack that night. Normally, he reserved all his man butter for Josie, but Alva really was something else and only looked more desirable with two black eyes, a cracked cheekbone, and a dislocated jaw. He hadn't planned on raping her, but what was a man to do when she looked like that? *Fucking slut.*

Royce took the rebellious couple back to the club, where they were never seen upstairs again. Bombshell steak soaked in mint urine was served for the next month and was a best seller on the menu, while Simon was eaten alive by his co-workers.

His colleagues had protested, as Simon was an important member of their team and well liked among his peers, but everyone had to learn. The giant pharmaceutical company had no choice but to comply, otherwise all Golden Cumpuss privileges would be revoked, and a powerful enemy made.

It didn't matter how big you were; the elite club had some insanely powerful and ridiculous connections. The influence they swayed was baffling. They could make your life hell. Everything they promised could happen, would undoubtedly happen if you crossed them. Everyone learnt their lesson that day…

... Except Detective Royce Miller, it seemed, as now he was planning on making off with their property too, despite knowing the dire consequences first hand.

*

Royce spent the next four and a half months doing all the things he was meant to do. He'd fallen back in line as far as The Golden Cumpuss was concerned. He made the regular delivers of worthless human sacrifice to the club and paid his almost daily visits to Josie. They'd even increased his discount to eighty percent from his normal sixty, while bumping up his per-shipment bonus.

In any other circumstance Royce would consider it a win. But not this one.

He'd started putting the idea into Josie's head about life beyond the club. He was incredibly subtle at first, talking about places he'd been, adventures he'd gone on. Just dangling the idea of there being a whole wide world out there for her to see, while guzzling her piss and fucking the pregnant beauty with extra vigour as he tried to hurt her experienced young cunt. *He was still unreasonably annoyed at her for not protesting the decision.*

Josie would sometimes react with jealously, wishing she could go to the places he mentioned. See the sights of Rome, or eat the delicious French food without knowing she'd have to shit it inside someone's mouth afterwards.

That's when Royce would push his agenda. Unlike

Alva, who was always her own person and free spirit even when she became The Golden Cumpuss's property, Josie knew no other life. They looked after her here and her daily debasement was the norm. She'd been institutionalised, and Royce had been part of the programming. He was as much to blame as anyone, which is why he was patient with her despite the hate fucks. Patience was a quality he didn't normally process, but she was worth it, and so too would be the tasty kid.

He couldn't have Josie raise any alarms, or act differently. The club might already consider her a flight risk being pregnant. While most of the girls gladly turned over their infants for a massive bonus, Josie wasn't most girls. She was loyal. She may well have been a freak in many senses of the word, but the girl still had heart. She was sweet. Somehow not broken, despite spending a life puking, pissing, and shitting, for the entertainment of others.

Royce needed her to know that she'd be safe with him if they left together. He needed her to know that he'd always look out for her, and there was life outside The Golden Cumpuss. And, most importantly, he needed to eat that fucking kid, so would tell her anything to believe in such dreams.

Progress had been slow over the months, as Royce saw less of Josie with the sweat licker demanding more of her time… but he felt like he'd gotten through to her. She'd started accepting his wacky notion of escape. They never used that word out loud, but they whispered about taking a vacation more and more. Started planning trips in their minds, with the understanding that it could become a reality. Everything was kept on the hush hush and Josie never shared any of these desires with the other bitches at the club or complex, but their excitement grew.

With Josie on board, Royce now needed to finalise the other part of his outrageously audacious plan.

The easiest way for them to escape The Golden Cumpuss was for there not to be a Golden Cumpuss left to chase them. For that, he called upon the long reaching arm of the force. He'd convinced the Commissioner to put him in charge of a crack team that was going to bring the human-trafficking scumbags down, and end their disgusting depraved institute. He had mountains of evidence against them. Every incriminating piece imaginable from photos to documentation, from bank statements, to the names and faces of all the players. Times, shipping numbers, licence plates. All the ID's and histories of the staff and guys and girls who worked the upper floor. Everything. And it all conveniently left his name out of it.

His team consisted of officers who knew what he was up to, even if the dumb-witted brass above him didn't. He only selected men devoted to him, guys who owed him, and whom he could reward handsomely. They were loyal to a fault, either manipulated by Royce, or just evil cunts ready to serve their foul master.

When this all went down they'd be heroes, be able to take their pick of whatever riches they desired. All they had to do was follow Royce into battle.

And it would be a battle. The Golden Cumpuss wasn't the sort of place you could march into with arrest warrants. They had judges in their pockets and spies everywhere. Everything had to be on the down-low, until it was time to strike. Then they'd take their superior firepower and raid the elite club, making sure to kill anyone who could pin the trafficking on Royce, while leaving enough leftover to take the fall.

Yes, his name would come up a lot; he was a regular there. But he would deny everything. Or he'd tell them he'd been undercover. He was Detective Royce fucking Miller; they'd have no choice but to take his word for it. What else were they going to do? Disgrace a super cop? In an election year? Not a fucking chance.

He could get away with this, if he killed the right people, and Detective Royce Miller always killed the right people.

*

Josie was ready to burst the day Royce finally made his move. She'd been pulled from the floor a week beforehand and taken to the complex until the meal was born.

While others had literally given birth to an audience of degenerates ready to eat whatever ever mess was left over, Josie's baby was worth too much for such gimmicks. *Birth Night would have to wait for the next girl who spread her legs and pushed one out.*

It had been a busy month leading to the final rest

period before she'd briefly become a mum. Everyone wanted the fuck the fat chick. To see if their dicks could poke the little critter in the face while it rested comfortably inside its mummie's tummy. They wanted to taste her puke and squeeze her pregnant tits. They wanted pregnant cheesy chips to be shat from her glorious ass, *that was her dining specialty, as she'd been craving it nonstop*. Whether it tasted remotely like cheesy chips coming out of that end was neither here nor there; it was the action of it that brought the excitement. She'd seen more brown toothed smiles the last month than the last year combined. For the rich and powerful, this was another way to debase and humiliate her, to make her feel less than human, even though they were the ones feeding on her waste. All it meant for Josie was more money.

Another reason to pull her from the floor was to make sure that, when her water broke, it was caught. Not a drop was to go to waste. Which meant Josie had a bodyguard with a bucket, which was an amusing sight to her. But, again, it would fetch a high price, *like everything else at the club*. The finest example of a recycling program known to man. Nothing wasted. Everything reusable. A perfect flawless system, *in their eyes*. If it wasn't all so unsavoury, they'd be up for environmental awards.

She hadn't wanted to know whether it was a boy or girl. Didn't care. As callous as it seemed, the less she knew about the doomed baby, the better, unless Royce's insane plan actually worked.

She wouldn't allow herself such thoughts, though; best

to see how things played out before getting carried away with wild dreams. Even then, it wouldn't matter; she'd have her freedom, but the kid would last an extra day at best.

One way or another the little bugger was going to get eaten; that was just its undeniable fate.

Still, when the doctor let slip it was going to be a boy, she couldn't help but wonder what sort of life it could have led, given a fighting chance to live.

Only a brief wonder though. The kid wasn't going to get that chance.

*

Royce's kill squad was ready. All armed to the teeth like they were going to overthrow some backwater dictatorship, they planned to fucking blitz the place, both the club and complex.

They'd been divided into two teams, but as the buildings were attached there were various points where they could meet up if need be. Everyone had their orders and were fully prepared.

It had been months in the making, and now it was go time for Royce and his band of corrupt officers. Do or die, and he had no intention of dying.

By the time the day was out, he'd have Josie in his arms, and his delicious baby in his stomach. His team would either be dead or lauded as heroes.

Most importantly, *although with a tinge of regret, as he'd enjoyed the comforts of the torrid cesspool,* The Golden Cumpuss would be no more.

The two vans they'd packed into pulled up tight outside the building like a ram-raid and the eager group burst out, ready to fuck shit up and burn the place down. They looked more akin to mercenaries than law enforcement, and in this moment that probably was the case.

Royce lead the way with a fucking cigar in his mouth and a shotgun in hand like he was an eighties action hero. *This was his moment.*

Until it wasn't…

*

The crack team of bent cops were gunned down the second they made it through the heavy front doors of the exclusive club. Ambushed. Everyone one of them took a parade of bullets from the storm of gunfire sent their way by the awaiting elite security team.

The lucky ones died. The unlucky ones survived.

*

Royce was one of the unlucky ones.

He and five other survivors were dragged to the barbaric basement of The Golden Cumpuss, bullet-ridden and beaten. A fucking mess, but they wouldn't have to worry about that for long. While the dead ones up top would soon be hacked up and added to the ever brewing stew, the remaining six were to be tortured and made to watch one another suffer.

Royce knew what was coming, but the rest of his team were in for a nasty surprise. One that, had he divulged beforehand, they'd never have signed up for.

Drew got his dick, balls, and ass nailed to various spiked boards by the security team that had bested them upstairs. The boards were then repeatedly hammered, digging the spikes in further and making his whole body vibrate in a pain he didn't know was possible. His ears were cut from his head and he was made to gobble them up. After, they repeatedly punched him in the gut until he threw the ears back up, and then they made him eat them again. The process continued for quite some time. Once the ears had become nothing more than pissy acidic liquid, it was his nose's turn.

Thomas had his whole huge body stapled. Like death by a thousand paper cuts, but with a staple gun. After that warm up, he was beaten with spiked clubs, and had his asshole ripped out with a rusty hook. Naturally they made him eat it, while some infected slave covered in boils was held at gun point and told to fuck the recently expanded incredibly raw hole. Thomas pleaded for death, but it wasn't going to come, not until the slave did at least. Once the slave busted a nut in Thomas's former asshole, his head was jammed up there too. Luckily for Thomas the guy had a small head, but Thomas didn't find anything about the situation lucky.

Karl was fed to the rats. He'd barely survived the initial shoot-out, taking an impressive fourteen bullets, yet somehow still lived. He'd soon wish he hadn't. The rats were hungry little fuckers and dug into the various bullet holes sprayed over his body. They especially liked the ones in his gut as they found their way inside him. Eventually they ate his eyeballs and heart, but not before he'd witnessed the rest of himself being munched, and had felt the germ-ridden infestation running around inside. Little remained when they were done. so he wasn't to be served up like the others; instead he'd be added to the stew with the rest of the dead. The rats needed to evacuate his insides quickly, or they too would be thrown into the overused massive cauldron.

Floyd offered some resistance at first, keeping up his tough guy persona -- which had made many consider him Royce's natural successor when the time came. The security team poked and prodded the mishmash of bullet holes littering his body with various sharp objects, but he wouldn't scream in pain for them like they wanted. Then they had his arms stretched using an old school medieval torture rack until they ripped from his body. *Turned out that was possible.* He was then clubbed half to death with them while the hired detail haphazardly cauterised the wounds, during which half his upper body, *and somehow his dick,* was burnt to a crisp. He was already half roasted and ready to be cooked, but they decided to cut a hole in his head and skull fuck him first. His opposition had long since faded by that point, and he offered them the screams they so dearly craved.

Jimmy, the last surviving member of the team outside of Royce, had seen what happened to his buddies and turned white as a sheet. He'd only received two bullets during the one-sided gunfight, *by far the least amount,* but he'd soon be wishing he'd received the most and was already in the stew. His feeble pleas went unanswered. He told them he'd tell them everything, but they already knew everything they needed to know. He'd done the normal whiny bitchy thing about having a wife and young kids, but they didn't care. Just laughed. His cries were ignored and his tears collected in a glass for later. They remained unmoved as he pissed himself and nearly choked on his own vomit as everything got to be too much for him. Once that pathetic pussy display was out the way, they whipped the shit out of him and harvested a couple of organs, which they then started to throw at him like some macabre version of dodgeball. *He was in no state to dodge them.*

They'd have to eat this one quickly, the security team told each other, as the wimp didn't have much life left. Fuck knows how he originally made it on to the crack team, maybe he was Royce's retarded cousin or something?

Speaking of which, that only left Royce unpunished.

They wanted him alive and cognisant for his final damnation, but that didn't stop them having some fun first. The claw-end of a hammer was taken to the formerly larger-than-life detective's flesh, expanding several of the recent bullet holes while also creating some brand new ones.

All of which were then fucked. The executives of the Golden Cumpuss, *including Matthews and several of the premium gold card members,* each had a go at nutting in the new orifices. One fucked the inside of Royce's thigh, another his armpit. Matthews humped the space where Royce's nose used to be, getting all worked up before spraying his dong juice into the exposed nasal cavity. It was the first time Royce ever heard the guy raise his voice, as he triumphantly jizzed.

Another spunked in his gut, while the initial employee whom Royce had lambasted at the start of the whole baby thing jammed his surprisingly massive dick into Royce's shoulder, cumming almost immediately with a 'fuck you, you deserved that,' grin etched on his face.

They even invited Jurgen down to see if he could get his mammoth horse cock through one side of Royce's body and out the other, but it fell just short. The poor Kraut was left somewhat traumatised by the whole experience, but they paid him generously for the effort. *He'd done some weird shit in his time, but that was something else.*

After raping the various tender holes, they all ass fucked Royce and told him what a bitch he was, before wiping their shit-covered cocks over any wounds they could find, *of which there were plenty.*

The once almighty and powerful Detective Royce fucking Miller was reduced to nothing. Humiliated and embarrassed. Cut down, and fucked every which way imaginable, including some newly thought out ones. He didn't whine though. Barely made a whimper, outside the pain caused by the various insertions. Didn't plead for his life, or beg like a fucking pussy. He wasn't the cocksure arrogant bully anymore, but they hadn't broken him either.

That was still yet to come.

*

Before they took Royce to his final destination, the executives made a detour to a tabled area downstairs in The Golden Cumpuss.

There sat the Commissioner and several other high ranking officers, munching on the remains of Royce's team. Thomas and Floyd had been partially roasted and had limbs hacked off and cooked, while Jimmy and Drew were being eaten raw; *Karl being scrap and boiling in a pot by that point.*

The table was full of laughter and cheer from the happy patrons, but not from the disgraced and dismembered now former cops. A couple of hotties from upstairs were filling the guests' glasses with piss. It felt like a party atmosphere that would go long into the night.

The Commissioner raised a glass of Spanish type A blood type *(his favourite)* to Royce, as he saw the former beast being wheeled past on a serving cart.

A personal friend of the mysterious owner of The Golden Cumpuss, he had alerted him of the rogue detective's betrayal nice and early. They'd had ample time to brace themselves for the attack, hiring the best and most ruthless security team money could buy ... with the promise of some beyond-fucked-up once in a lifetime post gunfight activities as well. *Which they'd all greatly enjoyed.*

Just as they'd given Alva and Simon a night of hope, they'd given Royce his moment, opening the door with his team behind him and victory looming, before it all went to shit for the detective.

With the case Royce had built against The Golden Cumpuss, the Commissioner had all the details needed to take over Royce's side gig for them. He could slide in and continue the human-trafficking business uninterrupted and without delay. The gravy train would keep on rolling. He'd get Royce's sixty percent discount whenever he wanted to be indulged at the club too. *He was unaware of the improved eighty percent, but wasn't as greedy as the detective.*

All in all it had been a great day for the Commissioner. He didn't need the glory of taking down the sick elite club when he could join it and take Royce's share. Was just good business.

The resigned detective now knew who'd fucked him over, but it didn't matter. Sure, he was fucking pissed that it was sort of one of his own, but he'd have done the same and knew it. He should never have trusted the dick weasel, that was on him. Or, he should have feed him the wrong date and time just in case; that way the ambush wouldn't have been laying in wait. Hindsight being twenty-twenty and all.

The only real thing left going through his mind now was what a fucking waste it was that he wouldn't get a chance to eat his baby.

Which was when he heard the damn thing cry.

The penthouse suite of the Golden Cumpuss looked incredible, like a five star restaurant that had doubled its stars. As Royce was wheeled into it, he found himself wondering why he'd never been to this room.

Sitting at a beautifully made up table underneath one of several expensive chandeliers was Josie. Despite looking tired, she was stunningly made up, wearing a gorgeous green strapless dress with light make-up hiding the recent strains of child birth. She smiled regretfully at Royce. He didn't know whether she had betrayed him too, or whether they simply didn't know of her planned escape, but either way he was glad she was okay. He could die having one nice thought at least. One kind moment in his blacker than black heart.

Crying in front of her on a serving tray was their baby. It was a boy, naked and uncomfortable, but Josie made no move to comfort the thing. She glanced at it a few times, but it was clear she'd already detached herself from him and accepted his fate as a meal.

Only, Royce wasn't going to be the person who got to eat the little munchkin; he never was. Not when his eyes fell on who he now knew was Josie's secret admirer.

Not once had she ever told him, no matter how often he asked. No matter how much he'd begged her to tell him who licked the sweat from her pits and behind her knees. Whose piss she swapped in their mouths. Who she shat on and spread it over their whole body like they were at a day spa and watched as he scooped it up and ate it from himself until he was sparkly clean. What depraved asshole it was who spent *his* time with *Royce's* fuck toy.

Not once had she fucking told him it was the Goddamn fucking Prime Minister who was about to eat their kid.

He picked the little fucker up and took a hungry bite from his stomach, as Josie cuddled up to the asshole, finally cracking Royce's icy exterior.

"Don't worry," the PM told Royce with a hungry grin, as blood and viscera fell from his mouth, "you'll be next."

Congratulations!

It seems you've made it to the end of your journey in one fucking piece.
Reading all those disturbing tales of depravity must have taken a toll on your mind, body, and soul. How does it feel knowing you have successfully ensured your place in hell?

Well, just because you've grown numb to the fire doesn't mean your suffering has to end...

... We'll be back before you know it.

Until then, keep your hands off your cock and cunts.

Otis Bateman is an extreme horror/ Splatterpunk author.

Bateman has a no-holds-barred style when it comes to his novels. He can be reached on Instagram @otisbatemanhorror, where he can be found interacting with the horror community.

Bateman is an edge lord who probably shouldn't be read by anyone….

Stuart Bray was born in Louisville, Kentucky on September 11th, 1991. His first independently published novel was 'The heretic' released in 2021. Stuart was first introduced to extreme horror when reading 'The house' By Edward Lee. Since his first novel he has released eight other books in the extreme horror genre. Stuart lives with his wife and two sons in Salem, Kentucky.

Stephen Cooper is an Extreme Horror Author from Portsmouth, England.

Having previously been a Scriptwriter he made the move to books in 2022; and has no intention of looking back. His debut novel Abby Vs The Splatploitation Brothers Hillbilly Farm was heavily inspired by the Video Nasties, B-Movies, and Slashers flicks he loved. This love of 70s/80s cinema has proven to be the backbone of his writing adopting the motto: 'Extreme Horror, Inspired by Nasty Cinema.' for his Splatploitation brand

While not writing, Stephen has created a Splatterpunk and Extreme Horror YouTube Channel 'Splatploitation' and a Podcast, 'The Splatploitation Book Club' which can also be found on YouTube, as well as Apple and Spotify.

Printed in Great Britain
by Amazon